STAR WARS™
THE MANDALORIAN
ALLIES & ENEMIES

Written by Brooke Vitale

Art by Tomatofarm

Disney

LUCASFILM PRESS

LOS ANGELES · NEW YORK

SUSTAINABLE FORESTRY INITIATIVE
Certified Sourcing
www.sfiprogram.org
SFI-01415

P9-DNK-809

Meet the Mandalorian
and the Child.
These unlikely friends
are on the run across
the galaxy.

This is Din Djarin.
Most people call him Mando.
Mando was a foundling.
He was taken in by the Mandalorians
when he was a small child.

Mando is a bounty hunter.
It is his job to track down wanted
criminals.
Mando never misses a bounty.
He is the best bounty hunter
in the galaxy.

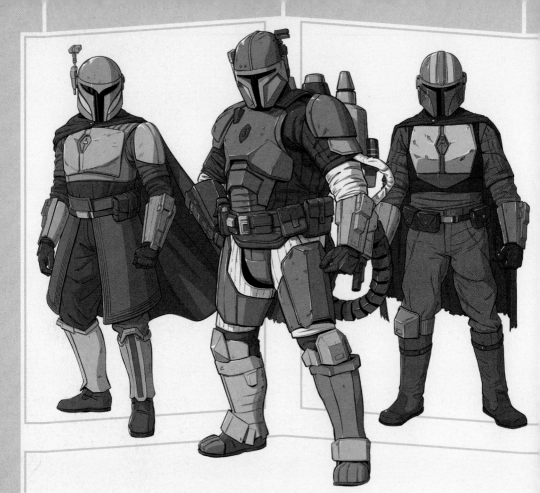

These are Mandalorians.
Mandalorians are fierce warriors.
They wear special armor
made of beskar steel.
They also wear beskar helmets.
No one is allowed to see their
faces.

The Armorer is a member of
Mando's tribe.
She is calm and wise.
It is her job to make armor
and weapons.

Greef Karga is a leader of
the Bounty Hunters Guild.
Mando goes to Greef
when he needs work.

The Client is a human.
He has no known name.
He worked with the
Empire and reports to
Moff Gideon.
The Client hires Mando
to retrieve a bounty.
He is eager to get his
hands on "the asset"—
alive or dead.

Kuiil is an Ugnaught.
He spent years enslaved
to the Galactic Empire.
Now, free at last, Kuiil just wants
to be left in peace.
It is he who helps Mando
track down the bounty.

Mando discovers his bounty
is an alien child.
Although Mando does his job
and brings the bounty to the
Client, he cannot forget the Child.
He takes the Child back,
vowing to protect him.

The Child is a member of
an unknown species.
Little is known about his family
or where he came from.
Even at fifty years old,
he is barely more than an infant.

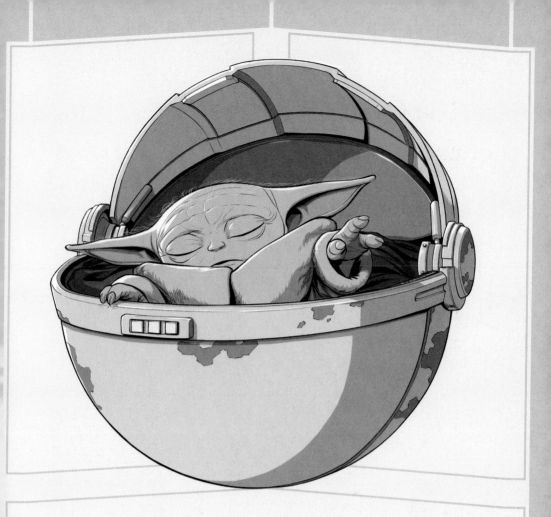

The Child is Force-sensitive.
He is able to stop creatures
far larger than himself.
He is also able to heal wounds.
Using the Force is hard on him.
He often falls asleep after.

Although he does not speak,
the Child makes friends easily.
He likes playing by the water
and eating frogs.

The Child is a foundling,
but he trusts Mando.
He knows that while he is in
Mando's care, he is safe.
Together, they form a clan of two.

Dr. Pershing is a scientist.
He works for the Client.
Dr. Pershing studies the Child
but does not want to hurt him.
Dr. Pershing keeps the Client
from harming the Child.

IG-11 is a droid.

He is also a bounty hunter.

IG-11 is not permitted to be caught.

If captured, he must self-destruct.

IG-11 is reprogrammed by Kuiil.
The new IG-11 is softer and kinder.
When Mando returns with the
Child, IG-11 becomes a nurse droid.

It is IG-11's job to take care
of the Child.
IG-11 vows to let no harm come
to the Child— even if that means
giving his own life.

Cara Dune is an ex-soldier
for the Rebel Alliance.
Cara is a fierce fighter
and not afraid to go into battle.

Cara meets Mando on Sorgan.
She thinks he is after her,
so she attacks.
The two soon make peace,
and Cara becomes one of Mando's
most trusted allies.

Peli Motto is a mechanic
at the spaceport of Mos Eisley
on the planet Tatooine.
Although Peli acts tough,
she has a good heart.
She comes to care for the Child.

Toro Calican is a bounty hunter
who wants to join the Guild.
Toro is only out for himself.
He turns on Mando
at the first chance.

Ranzar Malk used to be
Mando's partner.
Now Ran runs a space station.
When one of his crew is captured,
he calls on Mando for help.

Xi'an is a Twi'lek.
She is part of Ran's new crew.
Xi'an is easily angered.
She dislikes Mando,
but she will do anything to save
her brother, Qin.

Moff Gideon spent many years as an officer for the Empire. He knows all about Mando.

Gideon is ruthless.
He wants the Child and will do
anything to get him.
Gideon wields the Darksaber,
a weapon that once belonged to
the Mandalorians.

Mando and the Child have met a
lot of people on their adventures.
Many have become allies.
Many have become enemies.
And many more they have yet
to meet. . . .